ISBN   978-0-9876530- 2-4

Illustrations:

Antonio Parsons
a.parsons00@gmail.com

Published by

Daniel McCaffrey

P. O. Box 6280
Marion Square
Wellington 6141
New Zealand

mccaffrey.daniel@gmail.com

WHY THE WIND BLOWS AND THE STARS MOVE AND IT GETS DARK AT NIGHT

Once there was no wind, no clouds

sailed across the sky and the earth did not move.

It stood stock still and didn't spin at all.

It was a very strange world.

Half the planet had night all the time and

half of it had day. That's right.

It was all dark on one side and all light on the

other.

Most animals found this ok. Those that came

out at night lived on the dark side of the earth.

Those that liked sunshine had it all day long.

Everyone liked this, except of course cats.

You see even in those days cats liked to sleep

during the day and chase up a bit of dinner at

night.

But this world that was dark all the time

on one side and light all the time

on the other just didn't suit the cats.

Cats that lived on the dark side

were up all the time,

hunting dinner, stalking lunch.

Except it was never lunch and not quite dinner.

It was just dark all the time. Somehow it didn't

seem right to sleep while it was night.

 As for the cats that lived in daylight all the

time,

on the bright side of the world, well they never

felt it was right to hunt in broad daylight.

They slept a lot, as cats do when it is warm

and sunny, and got very hungry. It just wasn't

working out.

Day after day with the sun in the same place in

the sky. It was fairly boring.

So the cats decided they would do something

about it.

 You see cats talk to each other a great deal.

  When you walk down the street

   in the early morning

    you'll see the cats

     sitting out in front of the houses.

They whisper to each other up and
down the road. A message can go down the
street from one cat to another in just about no
time at all.

Street to street out into the countryside and
around the world. It was no trouble to work
out a plan. The cats of the world decided they
would get the world to spin around, to turn and
turn, to make sure that everybody got a bit of
daylight, and then some dark. The plan was
that on the same day at exactly the same time
all the cats in the world would dig their claws
into the earth and start running on the spot.
All in the same direction all at the same time.
And, because there are a surprising number of
cats in the world, it worked. One bright
morning, or dark night as it was on the
other side of the world, all the cats
in the world got out on the ground
and ran on the spot.

In the same direction at the same time.

And the earth slowly, very slowly, started moving.

The clouds moved across the sky, the sun moved

from one side of the horizon to the other and the

wind started to blow.

And for the very first time a soft breeze began to

blow the blossoms over the green grass, scatter

the drifting rain and brush past their whiskers.

And everything changed.

Sometimes it was night, sometimes it was day.

So that is why the wind blows, and why the clouds

scud across the sky. It's why night follows day and

the stars move across the sky. It's why sometimes

you see that very very pleased look that cats

sometimes have.

They like the night. Love sleeping in the day.

They know it was cats who worked out

how to make the winds blow, the stars

move and the mighty sun dance

across the bright broad sky.

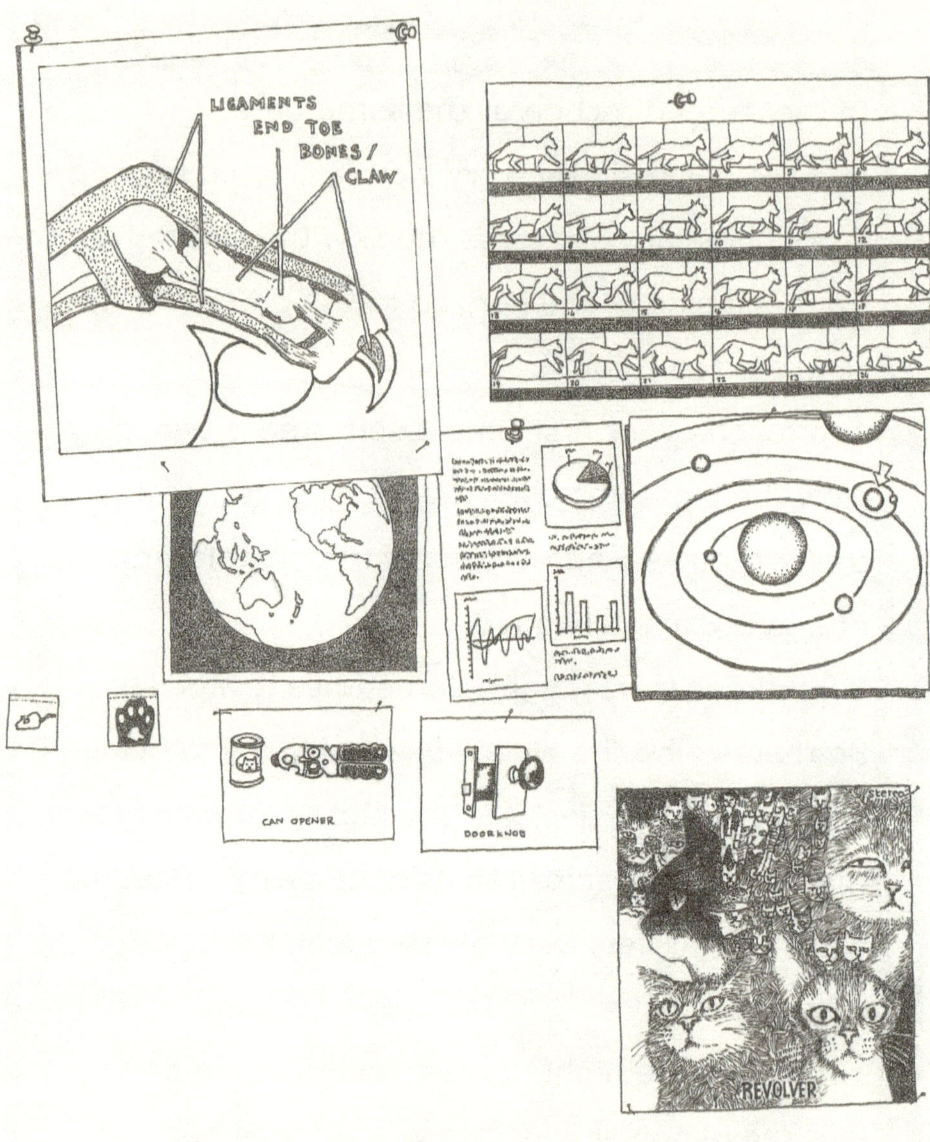

LIGAMENTS
END TOE
BONES /
CLAW
CAN OPENER
DOORKNOB
REVOLVER
stereo

WHY
CATS
CAN'T
SING

Long ago the people of ancient Egypt

worshipped cats. The reason was simple.

In those ancient days cats could sing like angels.

A few cats singing together sounded like a

heavenly choir, which explains why the pyramids

were built.

The Egyptians built the pyramids to listen to their

cats.

They would sit on the sides of the pyramids

and listen to their cats singing

on the sands of the deserts.

But one day, on the same day all over the world

the singing of cats changed to a truly horrible

noise.

It happened like this and it happened in Ireland.

You see Irish cats were great singers as well

better than the Egyptians.

Now, one of Ireland's finest

singing cats was Tunes McLurgan

He had a voice so beautiful

it could charm the small birds from the trees.

A very handy thing for a cat.

In those days in Ireland cats used to sing at the

great occasions of the little people, the fairies.

The fairies had their social occasions in fairy rings,

a round grove of hawthorn trees with a smooth

grassy centre.

There on fine evenings you could hear a fairy

fiddler, a few harpers, a piper or two and a cat

singing away. It was the most enchanting music

ever heard in all the world.

Anyway, it came about that Tunes McLurgan

was invited to sing at the wedding of the Fairy

King, a most important occasion.

Things were going well at the wedding.

There was singing and dancing and the fairies

were swinging round the ring

to some old fiddle tunes.

Going quite well, that was,

until Tunes McLurgan insulted the bride of the

Fairy King. He said she had the face like the

great goat of Queen Maeve.

Well it's hard to believe there was ever a fairy

with an ugly face. Or indeed hard to imagine a

goat with a good-looking one.

Be that as it may.

The Fairy King was enraged at this insult to his

beloved bride.

He immediately put a spell on all the cats in the

world.

From that day forward he ruled that the sound of

cat's singing would be horrendous and horrible.

And right enough, so it has proved to be.

All along the Nile people were driven mad by the

screeching and caterwauling of the cats.

In no time at all the Pyramids fell into ruins

and the people stopped gathering

to hear their singing cats.

And all over the world from then to now
a cat merely clearing its throat for a song
has people in a fury.

Still, though, cats try to sing.
Maybe they hope one day the spell will be
broken and their songs will again bring joy and
rapture to the people of the world.

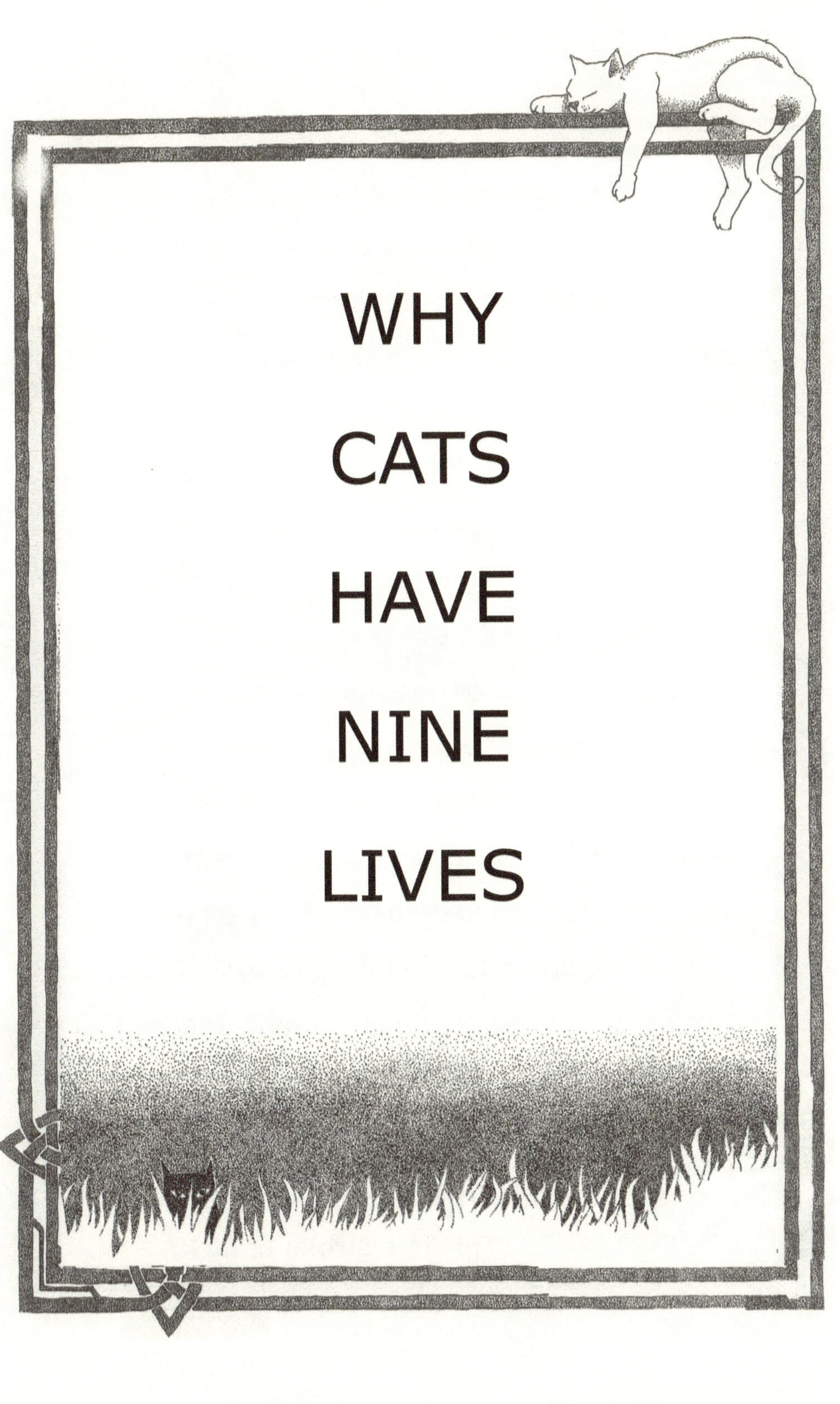

WHY
CATS
HAVE
NINE
LIVES

You know of course that cats

have nine lives. Well they do and they don't.

Let me explain why it is they do

and how it is they don't and when it came

about.

A very long time ago a cat called Dancer

was walking through the woods of Ireland.

It was a moonlit night and he was on his way

to have dinner with the fairies

in the small glens on the mountain side.

He loved a fine meal, a bout of singing

and the good company of the fairies.

He was looking out over a small stream

wondering how to keep his feet dry as he

crossed, when a loud shouting caught his ear.

Turning around he saw a small man snared in a

thorn bush.

"Well now," said Dancer to himself,

a Leprechaun.

This is a stroke of luck."

He knew that if you help a leprechaun

in his time of trouble he will grant you a wish.

Now that sounds easy.

But it's very hard to actually get a wish from a

leprechaun.

You mustn't take your eyes off him,

not even for a second. Or even a bit of a second.

For if you do, the Leprechaun will vanish

and with him your chances of the wish.

"Good evening to you good sir," said Dancer

"if you would grant me a wish I will free you

from the thorns."

"Ah fine cat you are," said the Leprechaun.

"Indeed, if you do that, a wish you shall have.

But could I give you a word of advice," said the

Leprechaun.

"There's a lot of people

that ask for a pot of gold.

It seems to be the first thing

that comes into their heads.

But think a bit," he said,

"You could die tomorrow!"

"What would be the use of all the gold

in the world with you dead and lying in a grave?"

"Well", said Dancer, "that's true enough."

"The best thing to ask for," said the Leprechaun

 "is a long life."

"Very true", said Dancer

"What is more valuable than life?

So a long life is a wish you'd recommend"

"Well," said the Leprechaun,

"Having said that, long life is not without its

problems.

"Nobody ever knows what life will bring.

You could go down in the world.

"You could be teased by cruel children

    or chased by the dogs of the cattle dealers

      at the fair."

       "Now that's well said and true enough"

         said Dancer.

"But what if instead I wished

for more lives than one. Wouldn't that be a fine

thing?"

"Ahh that's all very well" said the Leprechaun,

"but what if one of your lives, or even four or

five, were miserable?"

Dancer thought long and hard about this.

Living one life in misery would be bad enough.

Half a dozen might be all too much altogether.

"What?" said Dancer, "if you were making your

way through life's ups and downs and you met

with an accident?

Imagine now," he said, "if you had another

chance at life.

You could live on, wiser for your close escape, a

better cat. Now how would that be?"

"How would it be?" said the Leprechaun.

Why", he said, "you're a wise cat indeed.

That would be the wisest wish of all.

But there needs to be a limit or you'd live forever."

"What time is it?" said the Leprechaun.

"It's nine of the clock of the evening," said Dancer

"Well let's make it nine," said the Leprechaun, "nine lives for every cat."

And so that was Dancer's wish and that is how it is today.

It is why, when some cats have an accident they seem to get an extra life. They escape from situations that would cause any other animal to perish.

It's why people say that cats have nine lives. And it's all for the cleverness of Dancer's wish from the Leprechaun.

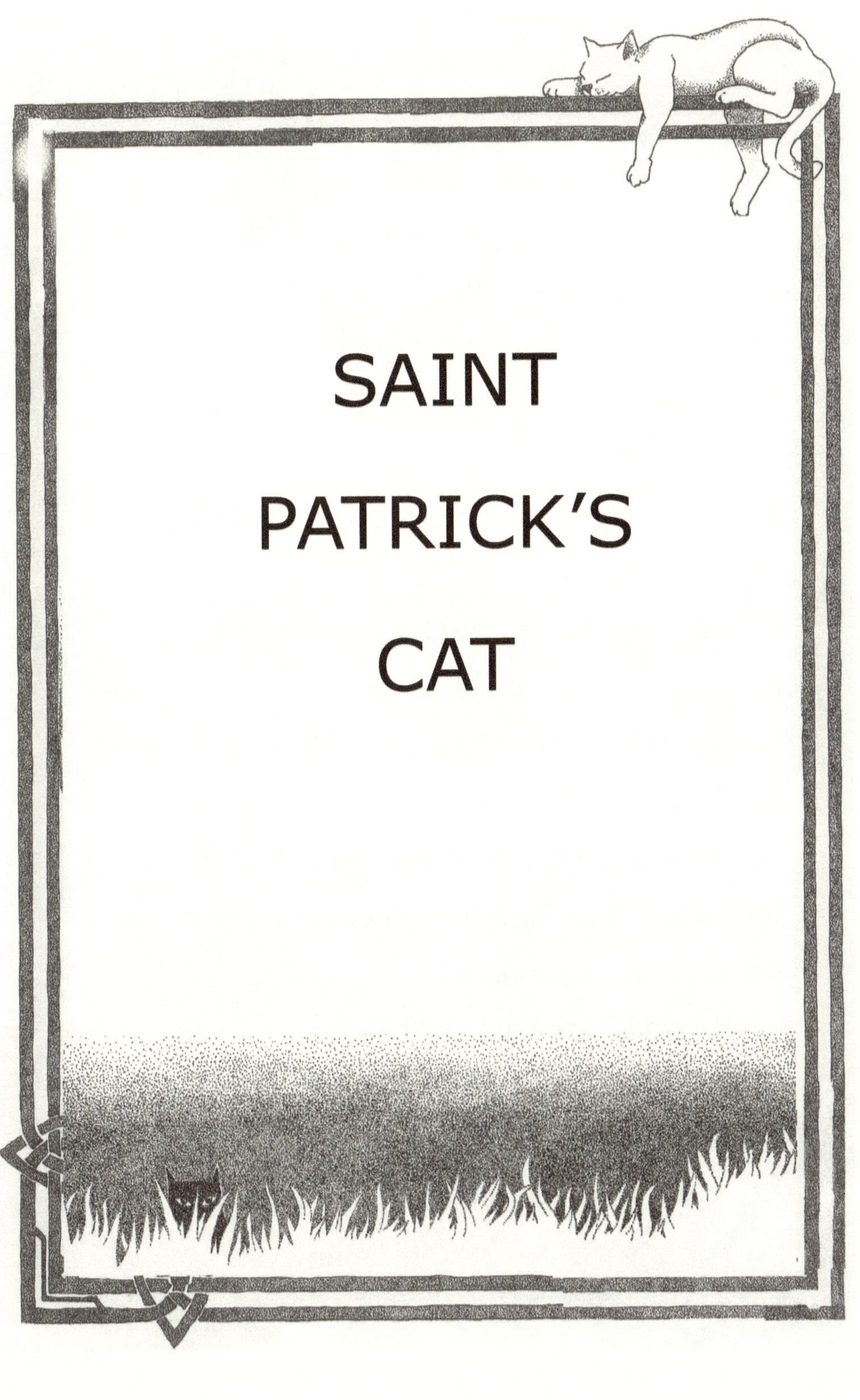

SAINT

PATRICK'S

CAT

When St Patrick first came to Ireland

as a boy he was a slave and spent his days

looking after sheep on the mountain of Slemish.

It was a lonely hard life away from the warmth

of his family and the laughter of his friends.

Patrick had a cat.

A glossy black cat of great bearing and dignity

called Midir.

He sat with Midir at the fire each evening as

he cooked his supper and said his prayers and

watched the sheep through the long dark nights

out under the stars.

Patrick watching the sheep and Midir scolding

the sheepdogs. Eventually Patrick escaped from

slavery and left Ireland.

He could not take Midir

but promised that one day

he would return.

Midir waited on the mountain

for many years.

One day a man came up the slopes

dressed in the robes of a bishop

holding a bishop's crozier in his hand.

It was Patrick.

Joyfully reunited with Patrick Midir followed him

all through Ireland as he preached to the pagan

Irish,

converting the Druids and making Christians of

the Irish Kings.

By the power of a miracle Patrick often conversed

with Midir. Often they would talk far into the

evening, as they had when Patrick was young

and minding sheep, about the ways of the

Kings of Ireland, the lives of the clans and the

churches Patrick planned to build.

One day Patrick said "Midir you have been a

        good and faithful friend. I have come to

            think well of all the cats in Ireland.

            Is there anything I can do that

                would make their lives easier?

Tell me what is the greatest tribulation

they face, the deepest hardship they endure,

and I will ask the most high God to ease their

burdens.

Midir thought and thought.

There were many annoyances that grieved the

cats of Ireland.

Icy puddles in the winter, sleet and snow

blowing   into their faces, the taunts of dogs.

At first Midir thought to ask Patrick to ask God

to change the dogs into rabbits so that all the

cats in Ireland could chase them round the

hedges.

Tempting as it was Midir thought it might not be

such a good idea.

Indeed it would never do. People needed their

dogs to mind the sheep, bring n the cows for

milking and guard the houses.

Besides there seemed to be

enough rabbits in the world already.

And then it came to him.

What the cats of Ireland would dearly prize.

"Dear Patrick" he said, "We are constantly

destroyed by the sliddyness of the serpents in

the barns, in the woods and in the fields.

They are cruel and eat the most playful kittens.

They make our lives fearful.

The greatest joy for all the cats in Ireland would

be to send away the snakes."

And so that was what was done. St Patrick drove

the snakes from the land of Ireland. Indeed to

this very day there are no snakes in Ireland.

Cats can come and go free from the dangers of

the slithery ones.

The small kittens of Ireland are forever safe

from snakes gliding quiet and wicked

in the long grass.

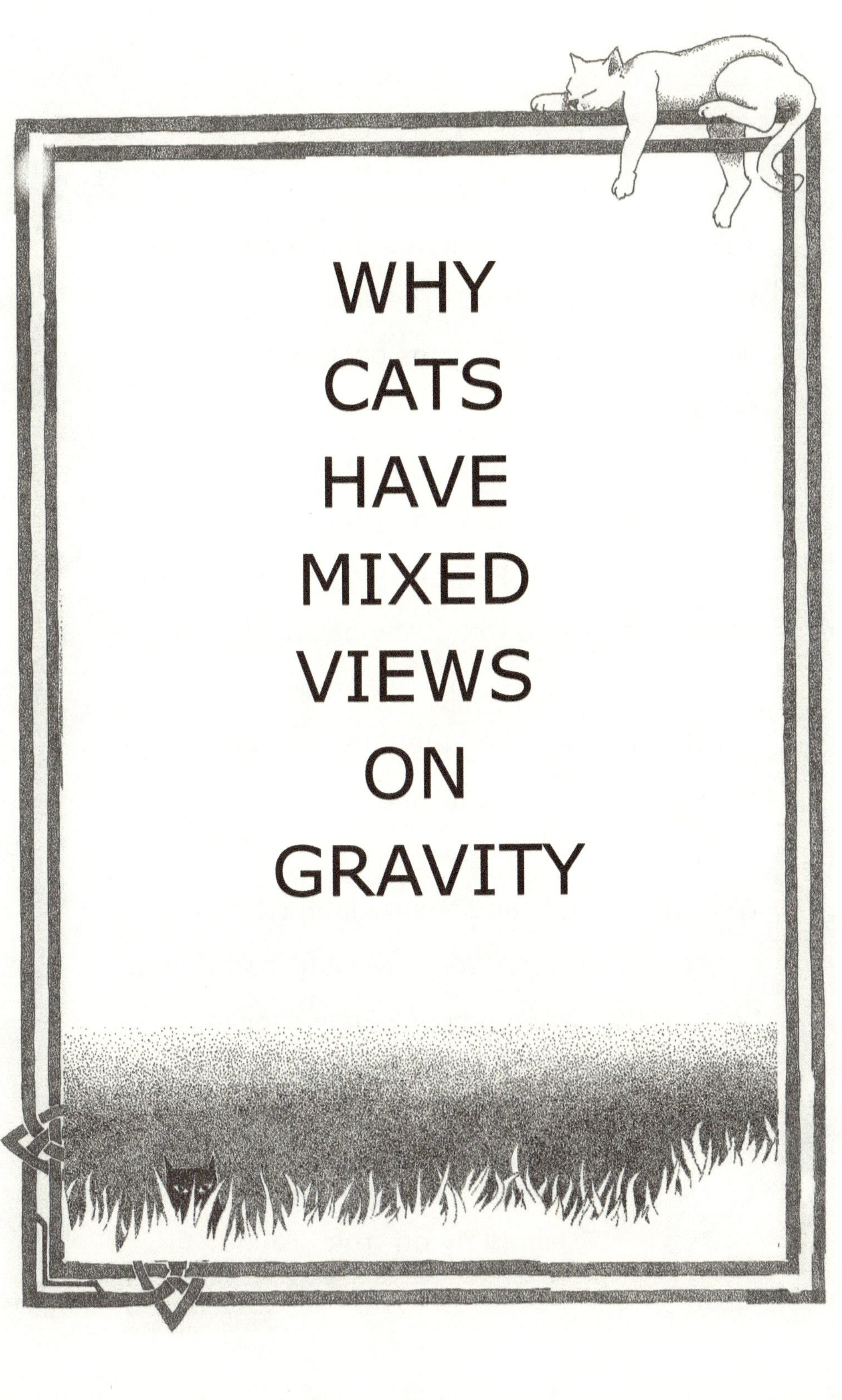

WHY CATS HAVE MIXED VIEWS ON GRAVITY

Cats often defy gravity.

They can fall great heights and sometimes walk away unscathed. The reason for this gravitational disdain goes back to the very beginnings of time.

In the beginning, after God had made the world, he put down his tools and said

"Look, I'm tired. I've been working hard all week. I'm having tomorrow off. It's my day of rest. I'll be back on the day after tomorrow. Check it all out and if anything needs fixing let me know. In the meantime you are on your own."

Well the animals and the people, (there were only two people for some reason) had a grea time on the Lord's day off. They checked out everything, and in the main, things were as right as rain. There was just one big problem. Occasionally everything would fly off the ground.

  You'd be walking along and next minute
you'd be way up in the air for no reason at all.
This caused trouble on a number of fronts.
The bears were upset by the fact that
when they grabbed a tree and pulled hard
they shot high up out of the forest.
The cows complained that they couldn't get
down to the ground to eat grass.
And as for the fish, well they had real problems.
Mind you some animals liked it.
The birds were very pleased.
"We can see everything that happens
and soar around the sky all day," they said.
Even some of the fish liked flying.
"It's such a nice change from being in the water
        all day" they said.
            As for the cats, well the cats couldn't
                make up their minds at all.

Some of them liked somersaulting

high above the trees and some didn't.

Anyway when God turned up after his day of

rest the fact that things sometimes flew up

into the air for no reason at all was the main

complaint.

"Well," said God, "that does seem to be a

problem."

"Look" he said, "I'll tell you what I will do,

I will put some gravity into the place.

Those that want to fly can have wings.

The rest can walk or swim, take your pick.

That is the best I can do at short notice

and I haven't got all day to argue the toss.

It's a big universe and you're not the only ones

in it.

And that's the way it has been ever since.

It explains a lot of things.

Why there are fish that fly in the air.

Why everything that flies needs wings

and why things stay on the ground.

Why the occasional cat walks away safe and

sound after falling from a ten-story building

without the twitch of a whisker.

You see, the cats couldn't make up their

minds.

They still wonder if gravity was such a good

thing after all.

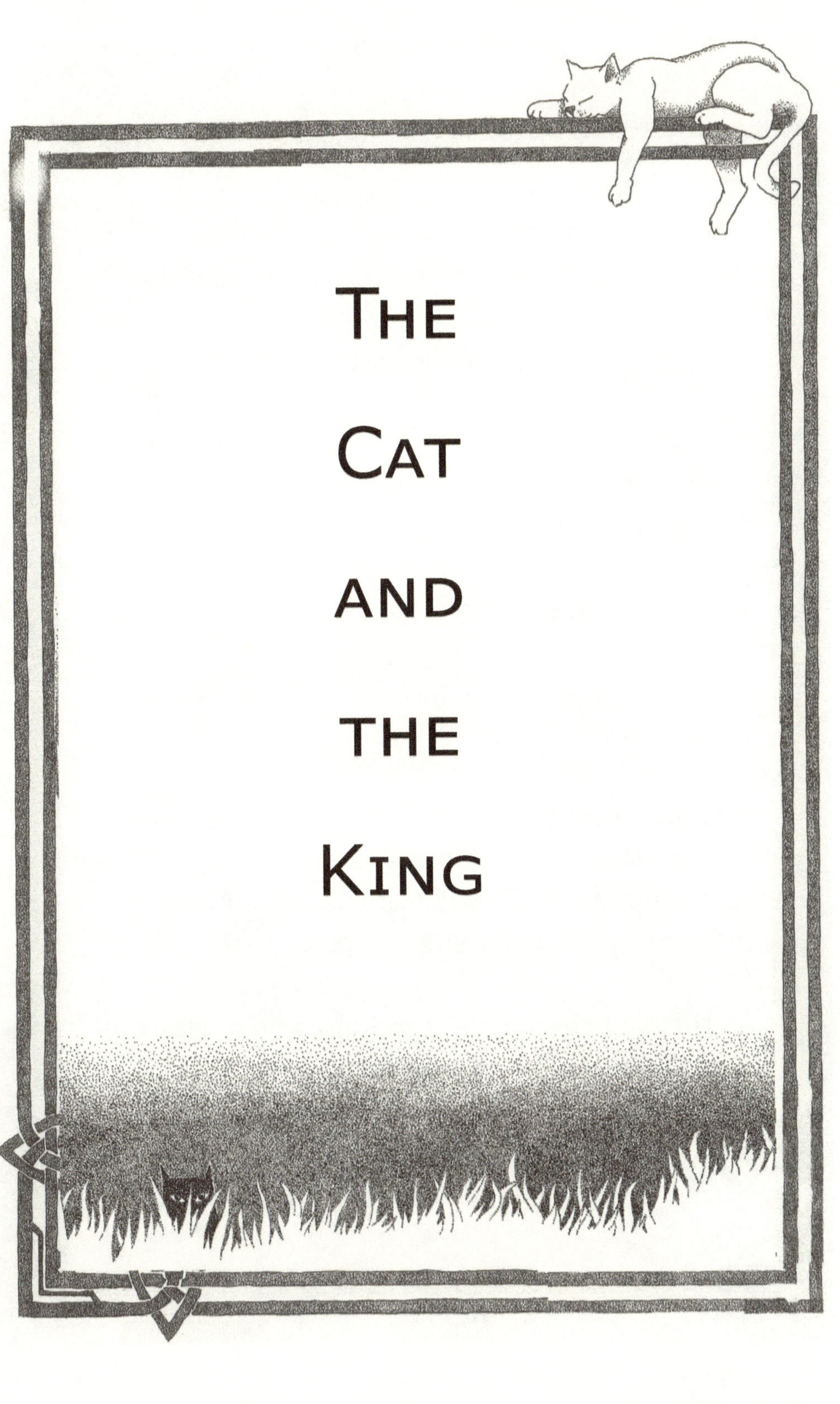

THE CAT AND THE KING

There was once a King long ago
who owned a cat, a fine elegant long haired
Persian cat of great poise and nonchalance.

In other words it was an uppity cat.

The cat wandered around the palace doing
whatever it pleased and generally bothering
the King no end.

The reason was simple.

You see the King being the King was used to
getting his own way all the time.

When he told the army to go to war they went
to war. When he told the Treasurer to give him
some money the Treasurer rushed off and got
the money quick as one thing.

All through the palace the King was in charge
   of everything and everyone.
         Throughout the Kingdom
               everyone did whatever the King said
                  to do as fast as boiling asparagus.

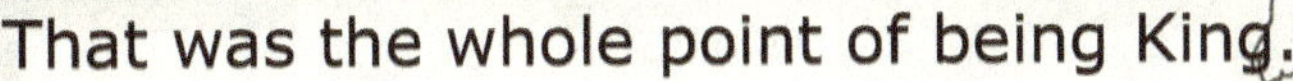

That was the whole point of being King.

People did what you told them to do,
Everyone that is except the cat.

Every time the King told the cat what to do it
ignored him, totally. It just carried on as if he
wasn't there.
The King was beside himself.

The cat would wander through important
meetings; brush against his leg when he was
greeting foreign dignitaries and saunter through
state ceremonies without a by your leave from
anyone.

Finally, exasperated the King announced that
next time the cat bothered him he was going to
box it's ears, big time.
All the wise men and the wiser women, the Kings
        advisors, were aghast.
"   It is terribly, really terribly bad luck
                to hit a cat, or even bother it
                for that matter," they said.
                It brings bad luck,
                    for ages and ages.

If you were to hit or admonish
the cat all the bad things that will happen in
the Kingdom for yonks, will be blamed on you."

You will go down in history as a bad King".

"All because of that uppity moggy," said the
King glaring at the cat.

"Yes indeed your majesty."

What sort of useless advisors have I got
thought the King, who cannot even best a cat.

He might not be able to touch the cat in anger
but if this continues thought the King this lot
are going to their ears boxed, big time.

"Well," he said, "Why can't we cart it off and
give it to some poor peasant far away who can
spend his time being bothered by this cat".

"Not possible your majesty,
     It would break your daughter's heart.
          She and the cat
               are very attached."

The King thought upsetting
his daughter would be greatly unkind.
He was not going to upset his beloved princess
over the sake of the cat.

"Well," said the King, "go away and do some
thinking and be back in the morning. I want this
problem solved"

In fact matters came to a head the very next
morning. The King came in to the throne room
after his breakfast.

There on his throne fast asleep was the cat.
The King was apoplectic, wild, angry and really
annoyed.

The advisors entered the room.
"Right", said the King, "what is your answer to
 this outrage and think fast or it will be the worst
for you."
        "What will people think when they see me
        giving my judgments, my orders
        and doing all that important stuff
            standing up while that cat sleeps
            on the throne?"

"We might have an answer,"
said the wise men and wiser women.
And sure enough just then who should enter
the room but the Princess.

She was a clever girl and she saw the problem
immediately.

Instantly she ran from the room and came back
with a bowl of milk and a juicy chicken leg.

Right away the cat woke up and jumping off the
throne followed the Princess and the bowl of
milk and the juicy chicken leg from the room.

The advisors thought themselves pretty smart.

The King thought they had just got lucky.

Actually he thought his daughter was pretty
smart. and would probably make a better ruler
than him one day.

For the rest of his days
the King took note of the lesson
of the uppity cat.

Instead of giving orders with the
understanding that a refusal meant a beating
with the lash the King started to make it worth
peoples while to do what he wanted them to do.

He got so good at rewarding them
for doing what he wanted that most of the time
people thought it was their idea. They were well
rewarded and the Kingdom prospered and the
King's subjects were content.

And as for the cat it carried on doing exactly
what it pleased, whenever it pleased, wherever it
pleased.

Except for one thing.

Any time the cat got near the King
it was always offered tasty titbits
        and bowls of milk.
            Which suited the cat just dandy.

The
Cleverest
Thing
Cats
ever
Did

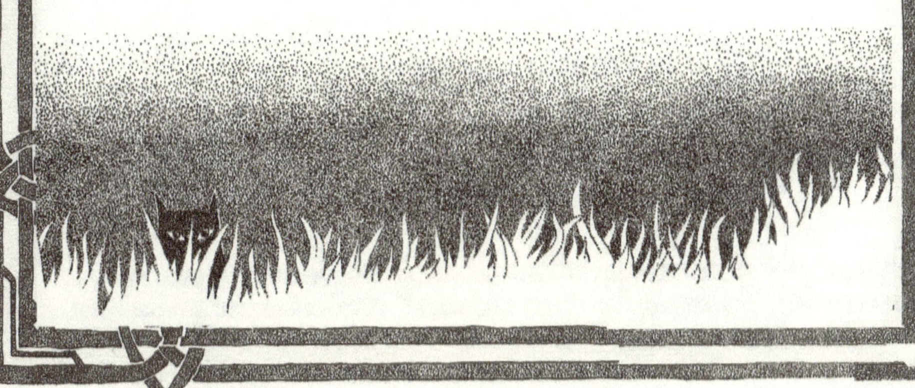

After you have read through
this book you will know that
cats have done some very clever things.

You will find out that they brought about
the modern civilisation we enjoy today. You
will understand that it was Cats who made
the earth move so the sun would cross the
sky every day and you will know how cats
managed to get nine lives.

So what you might ask ask was the cleverest
thing that cats have ever done in modern
times.

Do you know what the answer is?

Nothing

Yes indeed the cleverest thing that cat have
ever done is nothing.

This is what happened.

Some time ago cats
in the modern world faced a crisis.
Humans paid no notice but cats knew what was
happening.

 You might not know this but cats once had a
job.
 They were very busy purrsonages cats.
What they did was very important to humans.

They were the pest controllers of the world.
They had been at this job since the days
humans first moved into houses.

Mice, rats , birds and weasels loved coming into
houses and barns especially in winter. These
invaders would eat the food that the humans
had spent so much time and energy growing
and harvesting in the summer.

If these pests ate the food the humans might
starve. So the cats were very busy and
        important stopping these robbers
          eating the food.
          But then in modern times the humans
            invented all sort of new ways to
              package their foods.

They invented fridge's so mice
can no longer eat all the best food. They
invented plastic canisters and all sorts of ways
of keeping their food safe.

And they invented clever ways to deal
destruction to the rodents.

What none of the humans noticed was that all
this made cats redundant. That's right, the cats
were redundant, unemployed, no longer useful.

I bet you never knew that. The really important
events are those we never notice.

Of course the cats spotted the problem.

They knew the fact all the food was safe was no
longer their doing.

The rodents soon figured out they were
beaten by these new modern houses,
the vacuum cleaners that hovered
up all the crumbs, the snap
shut containers.

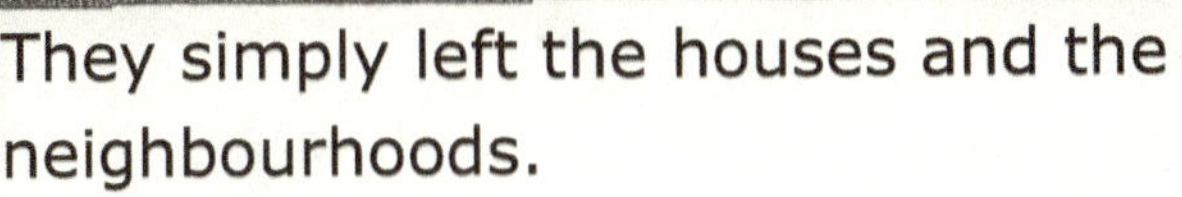

They simply left the houses and the
neighbourhoods.

Of course the cats discussed this at length.

One view was they could tell the humans that
they had done such a brilliant job and it was
down to them that rodents were no longer a
problem.
Yeah right said some of the cats.

The first thing the selfish humans will
do is say, job well done, here's a medal,
thanks a lot and heave us out the door.

True said the Scottish cats and mentioned
the old Scottish proverb, "Eaten bread is soon
forgot."
People only want to know what you will do for
them tomorrow. Not what you did for them
yesterday and nodded wisely as Scottish cats do.

We could get other jobs said some cats,
late night radio talk back hosts,
walking children to school,
all sorts of things.

Finally common sense prevailed.
Theres not too many jobs in the papers for
cats. After all Cats are small and don't have
opposable thumbs. The real skill they have is
dealing to rodents.

And if they did get jobs they would have to
pay tax and fill out forms and no one could see
cats descending to that sort of thing.

Some said well why not go on the dole but
it was decided apart from the difficulty of
opening bank accounts that it was beneath
their dignity.

Cats have a great deal of dignity.
Far too much its often said.

Then the clever thing occurred to them.

What if they did nothing.?

Quite right.
What if they did absolutely nothing
about the crisis.
And they did just that.

They made no fuss at all about the fact
 that they were on the employment scrap heap.
Not a word was said.

And you know humans have never really noticed
that cats have nothing to do. They don't notice
that cats sometimes get in 18 hours of sleep a
day.

Humans havn't spotted that cats have retired
and become the leisure specialists of our times.

So instead of being employees cats became
friends. They became companions and
playmates for the children. They kept their
owners entertained.

They stopped the tedious business of being the
midnight killers of defenceless little beasties.

So brilliant was their "rebranding" of their
position in the hierarchy of things
            that you often see very good looking
                female humans on TV whose main
                aiM in life is buying succulent
                treats for their much
                        deserving cats.

Of course some cats still have
different notions.

They sometimes bring in to the house dead
rodents, small birds or whatever. They are
not bringing gifts. Cats are not so silly that
they think humans want dead birds or mice as
presents.

No they are saying "look this thing could have
eaten all the food in the house,

I killed it. I your pest eradicator am still on the
job.

I am still a valuable employee around here."

But all in all cats handled the most important
crisis in cat history with a careful strategy of
doing absolutely nothing.

And they did it very well.
Of all the creatures in the world
none do nothing
so brilliantly as cats.

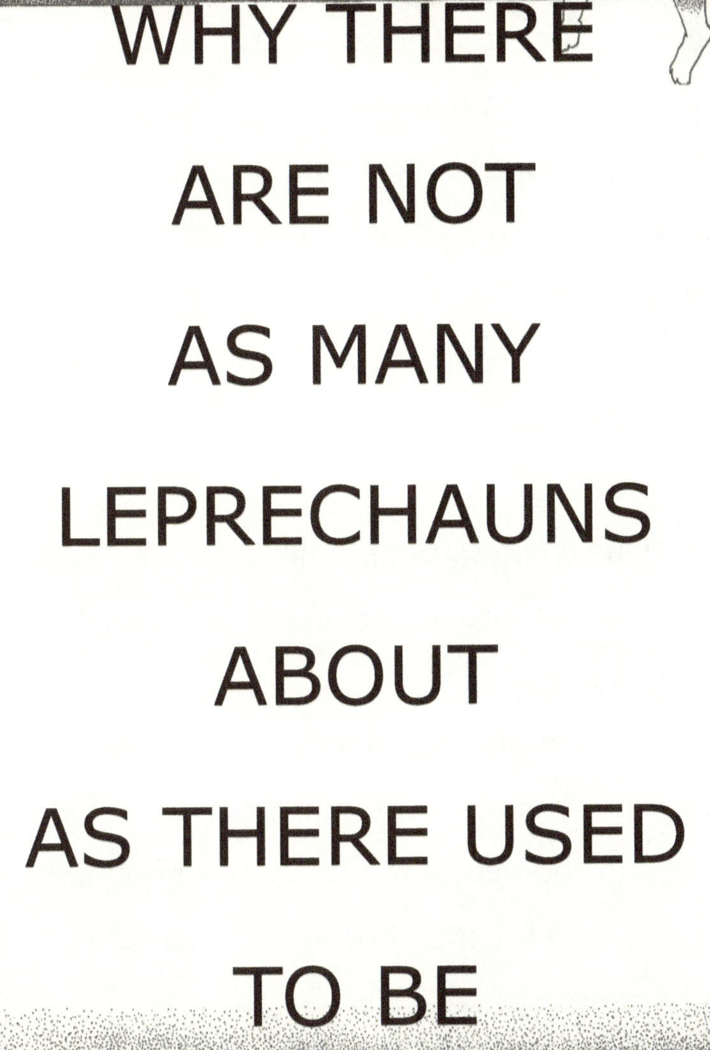

WHY THERE

ARE NOT

AS MANY

LEPRECHAUNS

ABOUT

AS THERE USED

TO BE

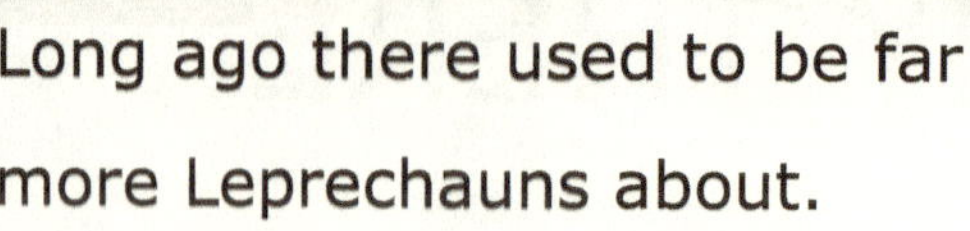

Long ago there used to be far

more Leprechauns about.

Crowds of them would ride out on their small

fairy horses to Ballyshannon and ride along the

waves of the sea.

But alas Leprechauns are a rare sight now-a-

days. There are reports of Leprechauns seen by

the roadsides but pay no notice.

It's usually when people have accidents. A

car swerves into a ditch and they blame the

Leprechauns.

The reports of leprechauns have more to do

with time spent at the pub than any sudden

surge in the actual numbers of leprechauns.

The reason for the shortage of leprechauns

is hammering.

Leprechauns, as you know, are the

shoemakers of the fairy world.

Fairies all need shoes.

Making shoes involves a lot of hammering.

There's leather to shape and nails to be driven.

The truth is the cats of Ireland were slowly

driven astray in the head by the hammering.

A cat would be stalking a mouse, moving low to

the ground with the deepest concentration on

its poor innocent dinner.

And all of a sudden the peaceful hunt would be

shattered by the sound of hammering.

Or worse, hammering accompanied by the

dreadful whistling of old fairy melodies half out

of tune. The mouse would race off leaving an

annoyed hungry cat.

Well even the most even-tempered cat would

be hard put not to take a swipe at the cause of

it's lost dinner.

In time cats decided that they would

starve to death if they could not stop

this constant hammering

and untuneful whistling.

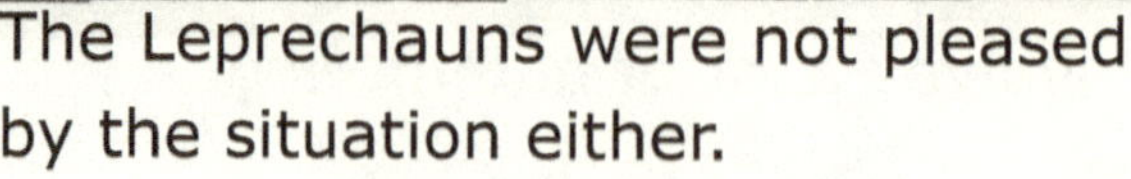

The Leprechauns were not pleased
by the situation either.
It's no fun sitting in the fork of a tree making a
pair of brogues when all of a sudden, you see a
whiskered monster comes along the branch at
you.
So the cats took a dislike to Leprechauns.
The Leprechauns took to keeping themselves to
Themselves and became very secretive.
They took to making their shoes in the wild
places out of sight of humans and away from
the dangers of annoyed cats.

So that's why leprechauns are seldom seen
abroad.

It's come about because cats like the quiet life
and an even chance at catching their dinner
and Leprechauns like peace and quiet
while they hammer away making shoes.

THE

WISEST

CAT

IN

IRELAND

The wisest cat that ever lived in Ireland
was Pangur Ban.
He lived over twelve hundred years ago on the
small island of Skellig Michael on the western
shores of Ireland.
He was the companion of a learned monk.
As the monk bowed over the pages of the book
of God he posed the questions that troubled him
to Pangur Ban.
"Why was this word so important? "Was it so
important a word that it should have a page to
itself? What did God mean by this phrase?
What picture could he draw on the page that
would bring these words to life?
Pangur Ban would furrow his brow and after
a while somehow the monk would have
his question answered. The island was
often invaded by the Vikings
raiding Ireland for gold and nuns.

Often, after a Viking raid, Pangur Ban would shake himself from the ashes of a dead fire and wonder if he was the only living being left on the island.

Would all the knowledge that was in the western world keep in his small head until he could tell a Monk the secrets of writing and the crafting of words?

But the monks survived and the task of writing and pondering on the mysteries went on.

The monks fasted a lot. There was never any table scraps for a hungry Pangur Ban. And wise as he might be he did not get to eat as often as he liked.

So Pangur had to think of clever ways to catch the island mice.

You see, they were not the slow easily caught mice you might find on the mainland of Ireland.

These mice were constantly chased

by seagulls and blown by the wind from the

sea.

They could leap a yard at a time and turn and

go the other way in the flash of an eye.

Pangur Ban spent the evenings plotting

cunning schemes and sneaky notions to catch

them Most days he had his fill.

So grateful were the monks for the wisdom of

Pangur Ban that they started including pictures

of him and his eternal quest for mice among

the illuminations of the holy words

of God.

If you look carefully in the Book of Kells

itself you will see hidden

in the illustrations

Pangur Ban

and his micely prey.

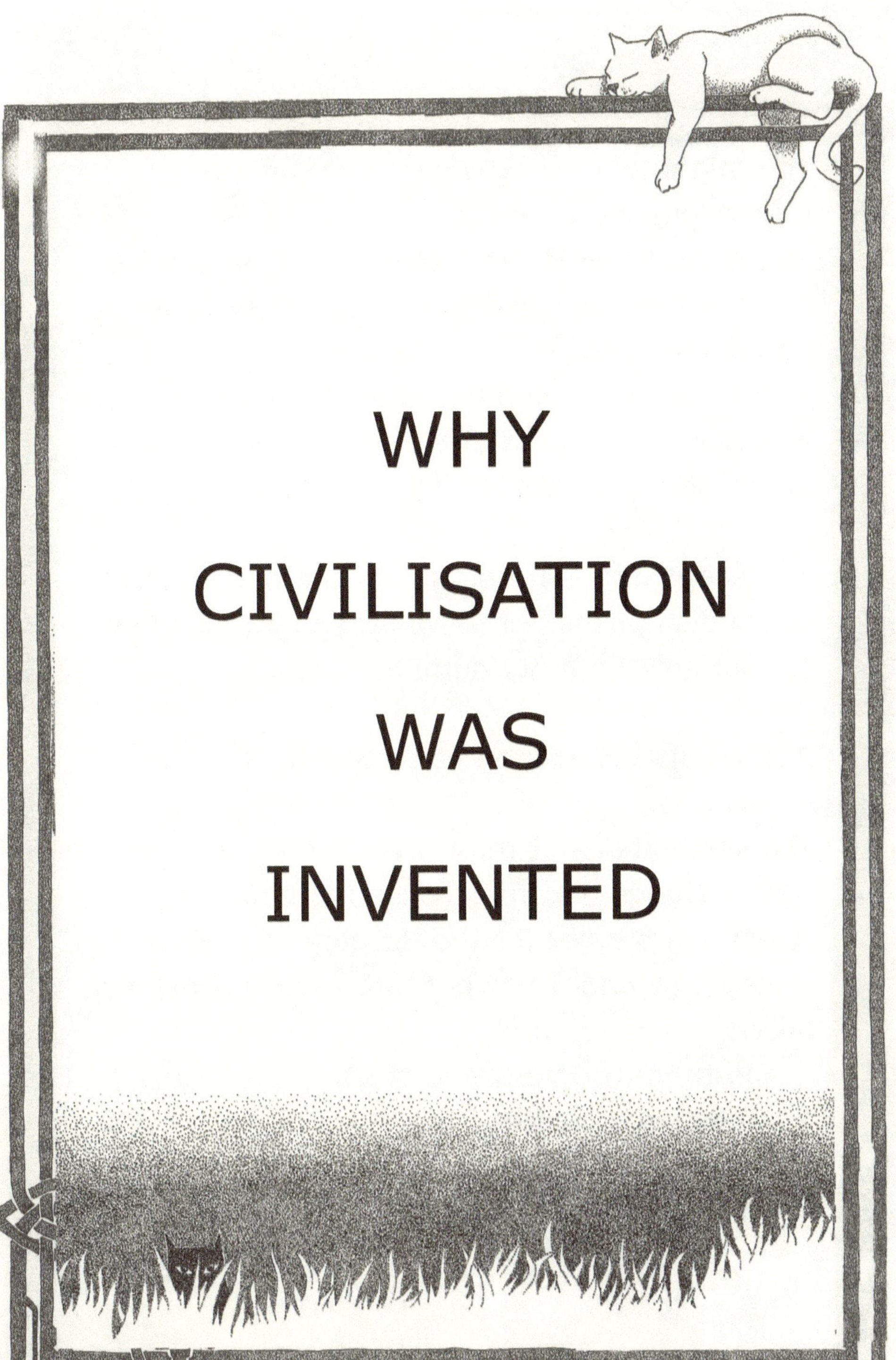

WHY

CIVILISATION

WAS

INVENTED

You might wonder why we have the marvellous world of today.

You could think it came about because people like comfort, or perhaps because they were curious. Not so.

The modern civilised world, with all its wondrous gadgets that we see about us, came about because cats like to drink milk.

You see, there is nothing cats like more than a warm dish of milk on a winter's night or a plate of cool milk on a hot summer's day.

And before civilisation came about, this was impossible.

You see, cats can't milk cows.

Before things became civilised a cat would reach up its paws for the delicate teats of a sleepy cow and try to get a drink of warm fresh milk.

And then trouble would start.

The cow would feel the tickling of the cat's paw and move a bit.

The cat would instinctively unsheath its claws. You can see where this is going can't you.

It would be days before the cow
quietened down and the cat could chance it
again.
And without milk cats get very thirsty.
When did you last see a cat drinking water?

Well the way cats solved this problem was
very clever.

They decided the best way to make sure there
was plenty of milk for cats was to get humans
involved.

If the humans started milking cows there
might be a chance that a smarmy cat could
sneak a drink of lovely milk.

People, the cats thought, were easier to get
around than cows.

All they had to do was mew pitifully
        and brush against their legs
            and humans could be persuaded
                to do anything a cat wanted.

Somehow people were inveigled
by their cats to try a taste of milk.

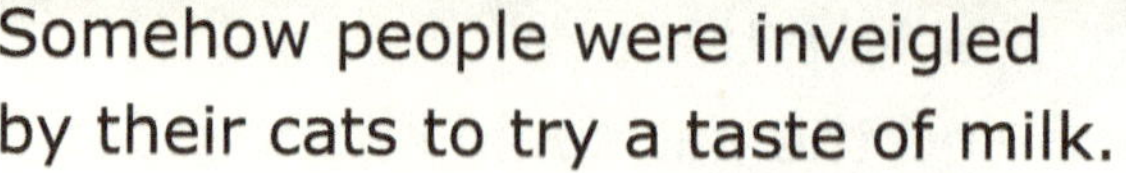

In their tea maybe, we don't know.
Well of course people liked the milk from cows.
They even fed it to their children.

And in no time the keeping of a cow or two
became the most normal thing in the world.
But they soon discovered that to keep a cow you
have to grow grass, reap corn, and stack barley.

Cows have to be fed through long winters.
You need barns, tractors, and milk plants,
refrigerators even.

So the people had to build the modern world we
see today.

So that they could give their cats some milk.

And that is how civilisation came about.

It happened because

cats cannot milk cows.

THE

LUCKIEST

CAT

IN

IRELAND

Fiddler lived in a pub in Cavan Town.

He slept in the warmest spot in the house,

ate all before him, and hadn't the bother of

paying rent.

Fiddler was so liked by the drinkers in the bar

that he could saunter along the top of the

counter lapping the creamy crowns of Guinness

in front of the patrons

and still be standing at the end of it.

But one day his luck changed.

You see, quite by accident, someone discovered

that Fiddler could pick winners at the horse

races. That's dead right.

He could slide his paw over the racing page of

the Independent and pick a nag

    that would romp home paying a fortune.

    How did he do it?

      Who knows?

It's said that years hanging round bars

with your ears open will give you this kind of

knowledge. Maybe he had the gift of foresight.

Well, you can imagine that in no time at all

he was a most popular cat.

Everyone in the bar placed their bets

on the horses with that certain feeling they

would win.

Of course the inevitable happened.

He was kidnapped, abducted.

Stolen away by people bent on making a fortune

from his gift.

He was never seen again.

You can imagine how much the drinkers missed

him, and their winnings.

Now nobody knows where Fiddler is today.

    But there is the odd clue.

        The occasional burst of prosperity

           in a small town that up till now had

           known desperate days.

Reports of people buying new fixings

and furniture where they hadn't a shilling

before.

Newspaper stories of bookmakers

lamenting a sudden run of luck among the

punters.

It's a sign maybe that Fiddler is being passed

around. or has been stolen again in the dead of

night.

His fortune was for others and to himself

brought nothing but grief.

Fiddler, the unluckiest luckiest cat in Ireland

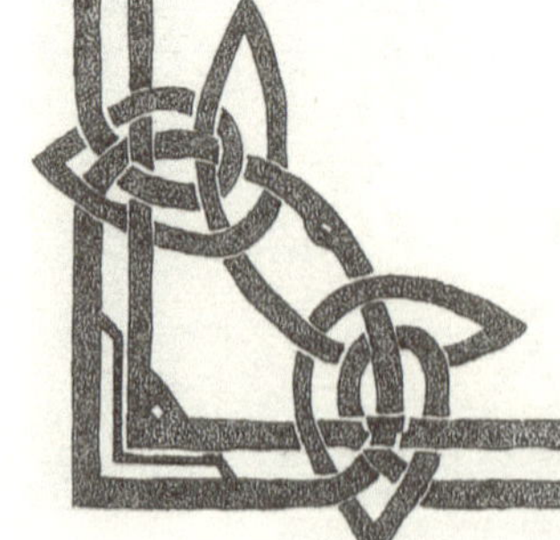

THE

BEST

FED

CAT

IN

IRELAND

You might think that the best fed cat
in Ireland would live in Gresham's Hotel in
Dublin or in the house of Lord Kildare. Well
that's where you'd be wrong.
The best fed cat in Ireland belonged to a band
of gypsies.
Well you say a gypsy cat would be lucky to eat
at all. The odd snared rabbit, a slow squirrel
and the occasional mouse from the side of the
road. Not a bit of it.
This cat, Nulla was her name, was the best fed
cat in the whole of Ireland.
She was as sleek as a salmon flashing in the
coolest lake.
You see the Tinkers' band that Nulla joined
travelled past all the "big" houses in Ireland.
And sure the people in them houses
paid no attention at all to a small band
of tinkers passing along the road.

Taking in the salmon streams of
Lord Killannin and the plumpest grouse from the
Lords of Galway it was a Gourmet Tinker's tour.
Not just the finest of food but superbly cooked
as well.

The son of one of the tinkers had been a chef
in the finest continental restaurants. So Nulla's
fare was dressed in the finest sauces of Escoffier
himself.

Now you know, and I know, cats like to eat the
odd bird.

Nulla had geese and gander, peacock and
pigeons, quail and ducks and pheasants hand-
reared in the best estates of the country.

A few peas dropped quietly in the evening by a
favourite path. In the evening light the birds
cannot see that every seventh pea
has a horse hair threaded through it.
A quick gobble and a quiet
choking noise is all that's heard.

As for the fishing.

A shiny piece of roofing iron set in a narrow brook with the shining moon above to make it easy for the gaff to hit its mark. Well you get the picture.

It was not all easy. Winters were hard. Nulla the cat and the women and children slept in the van. The men and boys slept under sheepskins out in the snow. But life was made easier by the fact they fed like royalty. So it was that Nulla lived the life of Reilly. She had boyfriends in every town in Ireland.

All it took was an invite to dinner at the campsite, a taste of the best food in the country a seat, by the warm glow of the fire, they were her friends for life if not longer.

WHY

THE

IRISH

HAVE

RED

HAIR

At the start of time in Ireland

people lived in tribes. Each tribe looked after

their cattle and their pigs. They hunted the deer

in the forest and caught the salmon in the seas

and rivers. It was an enjoyable life.

In the evenings instead of staying in their houses

they gathered in the centre of their land around

a big roaring fire to eat and sing and dance and

play the pipes.

Then, as now, the Irish loved to gather together

and talk and sing. The bards would tell poems in

praise of the King and about the lives of heroes

in the days gone by.

The pipers played tunes the people loved and

there was a great feasting and dancing.

      Later, as the fire crackled

        and the stars came out in the dark sky

        and the moon came shining

        through the trees, the story tellers

        would tell tales of Kings and fairies.

And that is how the people of Ireland

lived for thousands of years.

Now as you can imagine when the tribe

gathered by the fire some people sat closer

than others, some sat further away and some

grumbled out at the edges of the crowd far from

the warm glow of the flames.

And it was always the same pushy ones who got

close and always the same ones who were far

from the middle.

Every night, as the woodsmen brought bundles

of dried oak, ash and birch and as the turfmen

stacked up the sweet dry turf the same pushy

people crowded close to the fire.

In time it changed the colour of their hair.

The pushy bossy people who sat close to

the flames got freckles and red hair.

Those that sat in the middle

became blonde and fair.

And those that sat at the back,

well, their hair was black.

And this happened only in Ireland, for in the

other places in the world the people lived each

in their own houses with small fires to cook

their supper.

So that is why the Irish have red hair.

But there is one small thing that must be

explained.And that is ginger cats.

Why do ginger cats have such reddish hair?

It happened like this.

Ginger cats are pushy bossy cats and they

always sit closest to the fire.

And not just in Ireland.

In the homes of other countries most cats were

content to sit near the fire

and sleep quiet and content.

But even there the bossy ginger cats

got as close to the flames

as they could. And got red hair.

But it was only in Ireland,

in the inner circle of the great tribal fires, could

you see a ring of red haired people and their

ginger cats warming themselves in the red red

glow of the fire.

So that is how some people in Ireland

have red hair and why

the world has so many

bossy ginger cats!

Why Cats Have No Eyebrows

Have you ever noticed that cats
have no eyebrows?

None not even a tiny bit a twinge of a whisker of
an eyebrow.

It is possible that long ago they did.

Maybe big bushy eyebrows who knows.

But here's a clue.

They might have had them long ago but they
decided they weren't very helpful.

So they got rid of them.

If you watch cats a lot you notice they are
always licking the back of their paws and
rubbing them over the top of their eyes.

They have been doing this for thousands of
years. And it has worked.

So thats how cats
got rid of their eyebrows.

But why would they want to do that?
The reason is simple. Eyebrows are
very expressive. They tell people a lot about
what you are thinking.
Now as you know cats like to be inscrutable.
Mysterious even.

It's very difficult to tell what a cat is thinking
from its expression. But not from it's eyebrows
because it doesn't have any!

Cats like to let humans know that they are
doing the right thing to keep them happy.
You can tell when a cat is content because it
purrs.
But a cat's face never lets on what it is thinking.

If they had eyebrows, mice and dogs could
figure out what was going on inside their heads
and what they were going to do next.
When a cat meets a dog it fluffs up all its fur.
        But the main thing it does is not do
        is look worried.
            Cats remain imperturbable
                with not a twitch of an eyebrow
                    to show they are in the
                        slightest bit bothered.

And Cats sit very very still when
they are hunting mice. If they had eyebrows
a sudden twitch would scare the mice away.

They like being mysterious. They keep their
thoughts to themselves.

They like to sit and stare for hours.

If they had eyebrows it would be so tempting to
raise an eyebrow ever so slightly.

Humans give everything away from their
eyebrows.

When they are surprised or worried or happy
you can tell immediately.

When cats sit in the sun, close their eyes, and
dream their dreams they like to keep their
secrets to themselves.

And that is why they have no eyebrows.

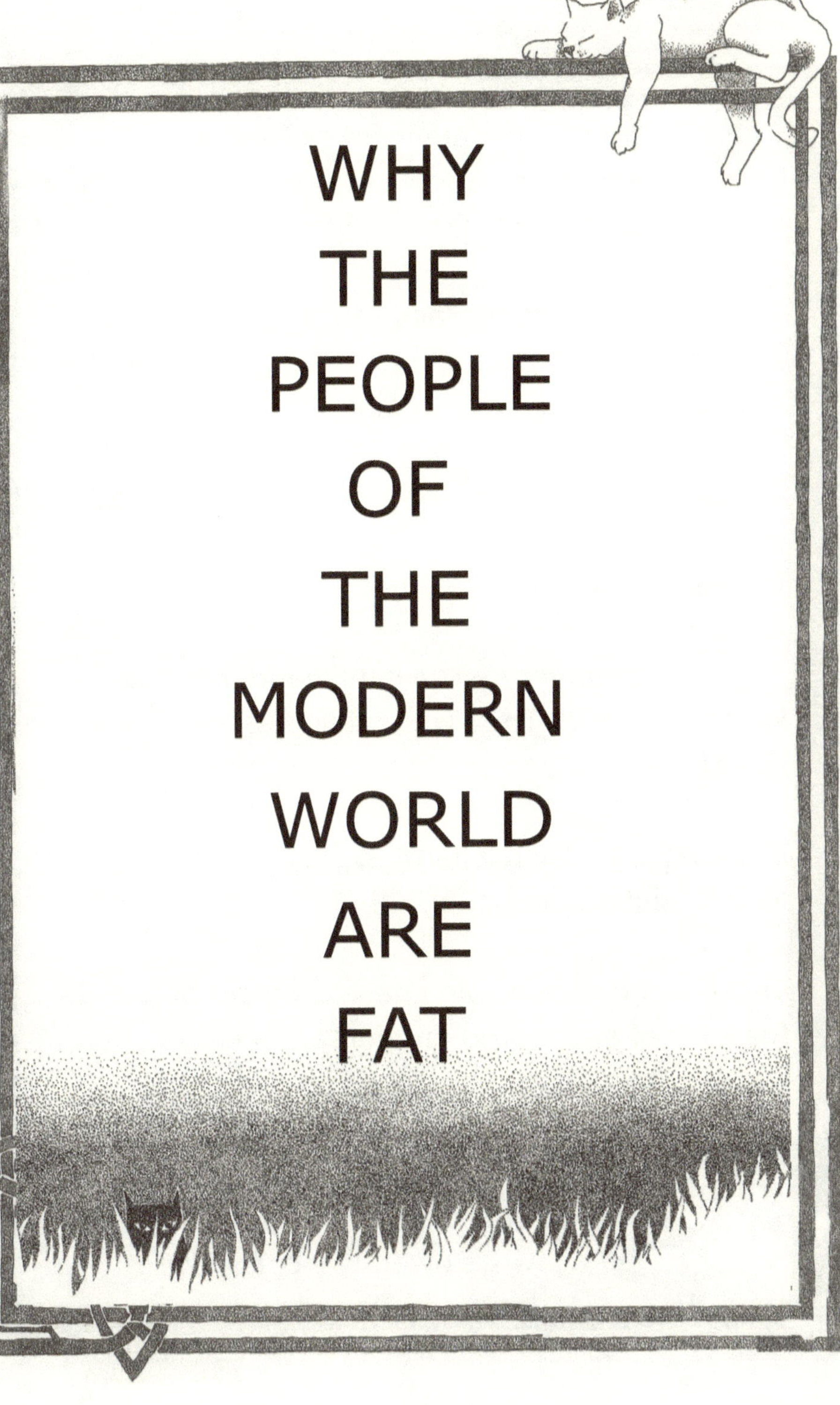

WHY
THE
PEOPLE
OF
THE
MODERN
WORLD
ARE
FAT

In ancient times people were not fat.
They lived in caves and went out in the
daytime scared out of their wits.

They weren't thin for lack of food. Not at all.
A fat mammoth chased into a bog would feed a
family of five for days, months even.

It wasn't the shortage of food that kept people
thin.
It was the exercise they got.

You see some very large cats wandered the
world long ago. They were called sabre-tooth
tigers.

They were just extra large pussy cats with
longer teeth than usual.

These large cats would chase a crowd of people
for a bit of sport, and of course, lunch.

The thin young fit people of those times
could easily outrun the cats.
The long sabre teeth hanging from their
jowls slowed the cats down.

Anyway the thin people escaped
and the fat ones were devoured.
This kept the local community fairly fit.

Indeed after being chased by tigers a few times
some of the fat people slimmed down
remarkably. Things were kept nicely in balance.
There were plenty of well fed tigers and skinny
people.

But alas as time went by and the people learnt
to grow barley and wheat for food they got fat
and lazy. And easy meat for tigers.

A diet of too many fat people made the cats fat
and they caught fewer people. So much so that
the sabre tooth tigers died out. There's not a
one alive today.

The result is that these days there are fat
people everywhere. Not only that, but they do
the daftest things to get slim.

The streets are filled with lardy people
for the simple want of a cat large
enough to chase them round
the block a few times and maybe
even catch a few for lunch.

This explains why often times you
will see a cat eyeing a human from the long
grass with a sleekit sneaky look.

It is thinking of those good times long ago
when its ancestors solved the problem of too
much weight on humans.

And thinking if such times should come again,
Cats would get a bit of entertainment and a
few extra feeds a day

THE

END